The Kiskadee Queen

EDITED BY
FAUSTIN CHARLES
ILLUSTRATED BY
LIS TOFT

BLACKIE

LONDON

General Rhymes

The rain showers down
The earth is getting cool.
All the birds on the farm are crying:
'Sheee-ooo, sheee-ooo, sheee-ooo!'

Yoruba/Nigeria

I went into a crooked bush
And cut a crooked stick,
I stuck it by a crooked yam
And took a crooked hoe,
I dug the crooked yam again
And gave it to a crooked girl,
Who cooked it on a crooked fire
And gave it to a crooked man,
Who ate the crooked yam.

Igbo/Nigeria

Don' talk — go ta sleep!
Eyes shut an' don' you peep!
Keep still, or he jes moans,
Raw Head an' Bloody Bones!

Afro-American

Mangoes ripe an' juicy,
Hangin' on de tree,
Mangoes ripe an' rosy,
Climb an' pick some for me.

Trinidad

Ham bone ham bone where you been?
Around the world and back again.

Ham bone ham bone what'd you do?
I got a chance and I fairly flew.

Ham bone ham bone where you stay
I met a pretty girl and I couldn't get away.

Afro-American

Counting Rhymes

One, two, three, four,
Johnny hiding behind de door,
Four, five, six,
Mammy catch him and stop his tricks.

Trinidad & Tobago

One, two, three!
Mother catch a flea,
Flea die, mother cry,
One, two, three!

Trinidad & Tobago

Mosquito one,
Mosquito two,
Mosquito jump in de ole man shoe;
De ole man cry,
De ole man cry,
De ole man cry like a little chile.

Trinidad

Action Rhymes

Twist about, turn about,
   Jump Jim Crow;
Every time I wheel about
   I do just so.

Afro-American

Jump up an' down,
Jump up an' down,
Hop an' turn aroun',
Like the grasshopper, green an' brown.

Virgin Islands

The rooster chews tobacco and the hen dips snuff;
The old biddy can't do nothing but he can strut his stuff.

Afro-American

If all the world's children
Wanted to play holding hands
They could happily make
A wheel around the seas.

If all the world's children
Wanted to play holding hands
They could be sailors
And build a bridge across the seas.

What a beautiful chorus we would make
Singing around the earth
If all the humans in the world
Wanted to dance holding hands!

Mozambique

'Children, children.'
'Yes, Papa?'
'Where have you been to?'
'Grand-mamma.'
'What did she give you?'
'Bread and jam.'
'Where is my share?'
'Up in the air.'
'How can I reach it?'
'Climb on a chair.'
'Suppose I fall?'
'I don't care!'

Jamaica/Trinidad

Juba this and Juba that,
Juba killed the yellow cat,
Juba up and Juba down,
Juba running all around.

Juba this and Juba that,
Juba killed the yellow cat,
Juba up and Juba down,
Juba clapping all around.

Afro-American

Clap hands for mama 'til papa come!
Bring cake and sugar-plum,
And give baby some!

Trinidad & Tobago

Auntie, auntie,
Thread you needle,
Long! Long!
Thread you needle.

West Indies

Little Sally Walker
Sitting in her saucer
Weeping and crying for someone to love her.
Rise, Sally, rise!
Wipe ya weepin' eyes
Put ya hands on ya hips
Let ya back bone slip
Aww shake it to the east
Aww shake it to the west
Aww shake it to the one you love the best.

Afro-American

Lullabies

All the chi chi birds they sing 'til dawn.
When the daylight comes all the birds are gone.
Chi, chi, chi, chi, chi, chi, what a pretty song.
That is what the birds are singing all night long.

Bam chi chi bam, they sing-a this song,
Bam chi chi bam, sing all the night long.
Bam chi chi bam, then just before day,
Bam chi chi bam, they fly away.

Jamaica

Rock-a-bye,
Don't you cry,
Go to sleep my little baby.
Send you to school
Ridin' on a mule
An' drivin' those pretty horses.
Blacks an' bays
Dapples an' grays,
Coach an' six-a little horses.

Afro-American

What are we gonna do with the baby-o?
What are we gonna do with the baby-o?
What are we gonna do with the baby-o?
Whoop him up and let him go.
Prettiest little baby in the country-o
Mammy and pappy both say it's so.
What are we gonna do with the baby-o?
Send him off to sleepy-o.

Afro-American

Thula, thula, mtwana,
Thula, thula, sana,
Thula, thula, baba,
Ubaba uzofika kusasa
Thula mtwana.

Zulu/South Africa

Hush little baby, don't say a word,
Papa's gonna buy you a mocking-bird.

And if that mocking-bird won't sing,
Papa's gonna buy you a diamond ring.

If that diamond ring turns to brass,
Papa's gonna buy you a looking-glass.

If that looking-glass gets broke,
Papa's gonna buy you a billy goat.

And if that billy goat falls down,
You'll still be the sweetest little baby in town.

Afro-American

Animal Rhymes

Me donkey walk,
Me donkey talk,
Me donkey eat with a knife and fork;
Tingalayo!
Come, little donkey, come!
Tingalayo!
Come, little donkey, come!

Trinidad

Sat little Renu with a bowl hearty,
Full of buttered, sugared chappati,
Suddenly a tiny mouse appeared,
Frightening little Renu dear,
Aside was flung the bowl hearty,
Full of buttered, sugared chappati.

India

Ole Grandpa Jake,
Changed into a snake,
He bit he own tail,
An' started to wail.

Trinidad

Monkey see, monkey do,
Monkey get in trouble too.

Aruba

The cuckoo calls, coo, coo, coo,
Don't touch the mangoes any of you,
For I am the mango queen you see,
Eating mangoes is for me.

India

Kiskadee bird, kiskadee!
Up in de tree,
Singin' sweetly to me,
Kiskadee! Kiskadee!

Trinidad

Through the jungle the elephant goes,
Swaying his trunk to and fro,
Munching, crunching, tearing trees,
Stamping seeds, eating leaves.
His eyes are small, his feet are fat,
Hey, elephant, don't behave like that.

India

Listen to the tree bear
Crying in the night
Crying for his mammy
In the pale moonlight.

What will his Mammy do
When she hears him cry?
She'll tuck him in a cocoa-pod
And sing a lullaby.

Ashanti/Ghana

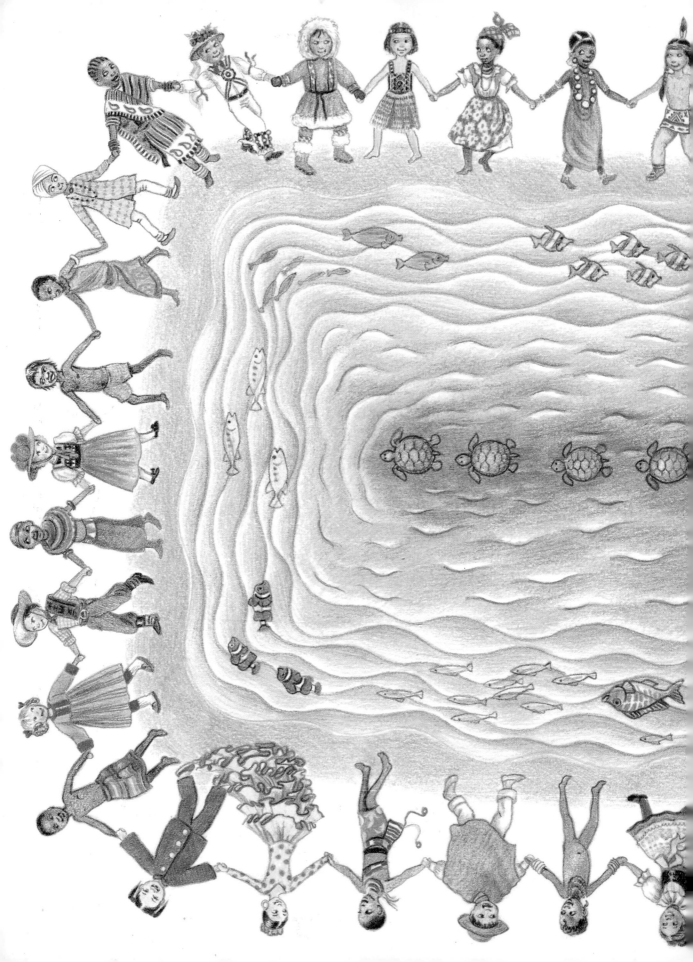